W9-BVZ-933

Dear Parents:

Congratulations! Your child is taking the first steps on an exciting journey. The destination? Independent reading!

STEP INTO READING® will help your child get there. The program offers five steps to reading success. Each step includes fun stories and colorful art or photographs. In addition to original fiction and books with favorite characters, there are Step into Reading Non-Fiction Readers, Phonics Readers and Boxed Sets, Sticker Readers, and Comic Readers—a complete literacy program with something to interest every child.

Learning to Read, Step by Step!

Ready to Read **Preschool–Kindergarten**
• big type and easy words • rhyme and rhythm • picture clues
For children who know the alphabet and are eager to begin reading.

Reading with Help **Preschool–Grade 1**
• basic vocabulary • short sentences • simple stories
For children who recognize familiar words and sound out new words with help.

Reading on Your Own **Grades 1–3**
• engaging characters • easy-to-follow plots • popular topics
For children who are ready to read on their own.

Reading Paragraphs **Grades 2–3**
• challenging vocabulary • short paragraphs • exciting stories
For newly independent readers who read simple sentences with confidence.

Ready for Chapters **Grades 2–4**
• chapters • longer paragraphs • full-color art
For children who want to take the plunge into chapter books but still like colorful pictures.

STEP INTO READING® is designed to give every child a successful reading experience. The grade levels are only guides; children will progress through the steps at their own speed, developing confidence in their reading. The F&P Text Level on the back cover serves as another tool to help you choose the right book for your child.

Remember, a lifetime love of reading starts with a single step!

For Julia G.
—J.R.

Text copyright © 2022 by Jean Reagan
Cover art and interior illustrations copyright © 2022 by Lee Wildish

All rights reserved. Published in the United States by Random House Children's Books, a division of Penguin Random House LLC, New York.

Step into Reading, Random House, and the Random House colophon are registered trademarks of Penguin Random House LLC.

Visit us on the Web!
StepIntoReading.com
rhcbooks.com

Educators and librarians, for a variety of teaching tools, visit us at RHTeachersLibrarians.com

Library of Congress Cataloging-in-Publication Data is available upon request.
ISBN 978-0-593-47917-9 (trade) — ISBN 978-0-593-47918-6 (lib. bdg.) —
ISBN 978-0-593-47919-3 (ebook)

Printed in the United States of America
10 9 8 7 6 5 4 3 2 1
First Edition

This book has been officially leveled by using the F&P Text Level Gradient™ Leveling System.

BAKE AN APPLE PIE

by Jean Reagan
illustrated by Lee Wildish

Random House 🏠 New York

Grandpa and I are planning a surprise.

4

When Grandma
goes out,
we will make her
an apple pie!

Goodbye, Grandma!

We rush outside
to pick apples.

We chop the apples
and mix in sugar
and spices.

11

We make dough.

12

Together we roll it
into two big
circles,
a bottom and a top.

We put in
the bottom crust,
add the filling,
and put on the top.

The pie is in the oven!

We set the timer.

Oh no!

We hear Grandma!

The pie is not ready!
We *must* slow her down.

Don't worry, Grandpa!

I have a great idea.

I rush outside.

Hi, Grandma!

Let's surprise Grandpa.

We can pick flowers
for him.

We pick
lots and lots
of flowers.

I hope

the pie is done.

We open the door . . .

26

"Surprise!"

We eat our yummy
apple pie and
plan which pie
to make next.

Let's try pumpkin!

31